THIS BOOK BELONGS TO:

_____

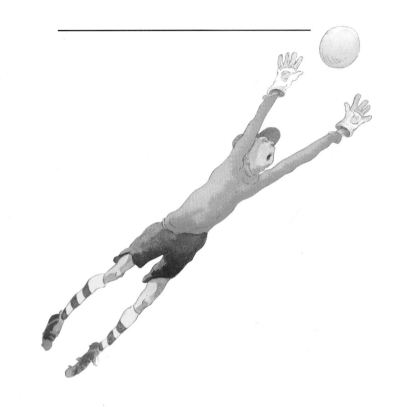

ww
li

pages from my sketchbooks— Michael Foreman

NEW YORK 1997

FUJI FOOTBALL     Japan 1996

YUCATAN    March 1979

Berlin Wall    1970

Siena . Italy 1996

Marseille 1999

Monastery at Singhik, Tibetan border. 1974

**For Colin McNaughton – and dreamers everywhere**

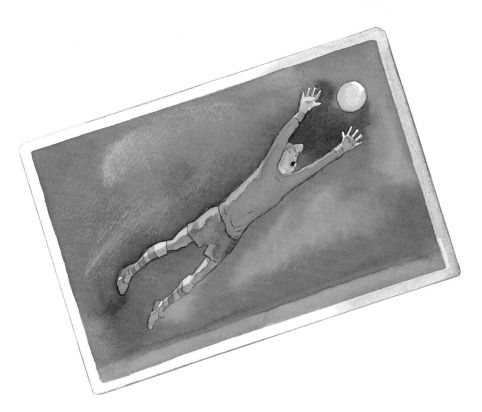

This paperback edition first published in 2009 by Andersen Press Ltd.
First published in Great Britain in 2002 by Andersen Press Ltd.,
20 Vauxhall Bridge Road, London SW1V 2SA.
Published in Australia by Random House Australia Pty.,
Level 3, 100 Pacific Highway, North Sydney, NSW 2060.
Copyright © Michael Foreman, 2002
The rights of Michael Foreman to be identified as the author and illustrator
of this work have been asserted by him in accordance with the
Copyright, Designs and Patents Act, 1988.

Colour separated in Switzerland by Photolitho AG, Zürich.
Printed and bound in Singapore by Tien Wah Press.

10   9   8   7   6   5   4   3   2

British Library Cataloguing in Publication Data available.

ISBN 978 1 84270 934 4

# WONDER GOAL!

## MICHAEL FOREMAN

ANDERSEN PRESS

It was a cold Sunday in winter, and the boy hadn't noticed the lads tie his bootlaces together on the way to the game.
So when he tripped and fell out of the builder's van that was their team bus it just made him even more determined to 'show them'.

They were good lads really, but he was new to the team and they always teased the new boy.

And when they ran out to start the game, he knew they all dreamed the same dream, the same impossible dream of one day becoming famous footballers.

In the second half, he got his chance to 'show them'.

It was perfect.
Head over the ball, balance, power, timing.
All the things his dad had told him.

As soon as he kicked it,
he knew it was going
to be a goal.
It was a screamer.
No keeper in the world
would save that shot.

Maybe now his team mates
would stop teasing him.

Then in his mind,
everything seemed to stop,
frozen in time.

The keeper seemed
to hang in the air,
and the ball hovered
just beyond his fingertips.

It was like a photograph . . .

. . . like all those
photographs that crowded
the walls of his tiny
bedroom, where he dreamed
every night of scoring a
wonder goal and winning
the World Cup.

He knew his dad used to have the same dream when he was a boy, and that he too had slept in a room wall to wall with heroes.

His dad usually came to all the games but this weekend he had to work overtime. His dad was not going to see the wonder goal. It wouldn't be in the papers and it wouldn't be on the telly. And his dad was going to miss it.

All this flashed through his mind as the ball flew towards the goal. And then time clicked into gear once more and moved on . . .

and on . . .

The keeper hit the ground . . .

. . . and the ball smacked
into the back of the net.

The vast crowd erupted.
He had hit another
**wonder goal!**

Just like the goal he had
scored all those years before
on that freezing boyhood
Sunday.

Maybe now, after such a goal, his team mates would stop teasing him.
They were good lads really, but he was the newest member of the squad and they always teased the new boy.

And anyway, he knew they had always shared the same dream of winning the World Cup . . .

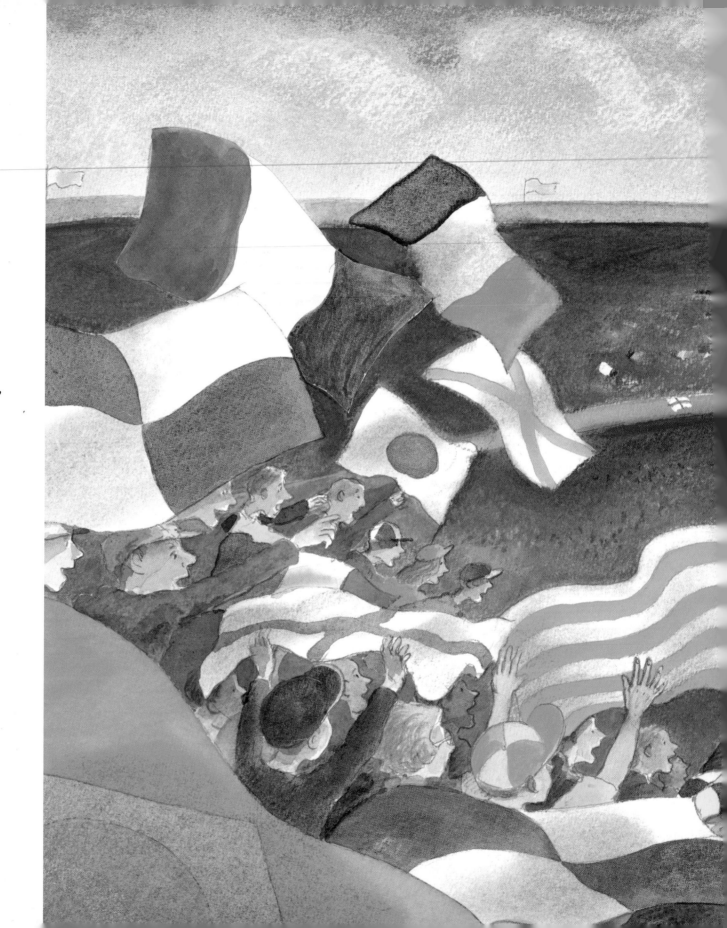

They hadn't won it yet, but he *had* just scored the first goal of the Final . . .
And this time it would be in all the papers, and on the telly.

And this time – *this* time, his dad was there to see it.

Soccer in the Straits of Malacca

Football in the City of the Dead  Cairo

Arabia 197_

Golan Heights, Israel
1970

School yard. North China, 1972

pages from my sketchbooks— Michael Foreman

me playing football in the snow.

# Other books by

# MICHAEL FOREMAN

9781849392198

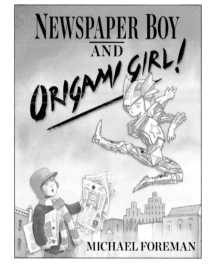

9781849395199

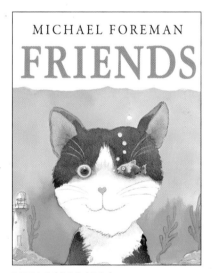

9781849394154

9781849392242

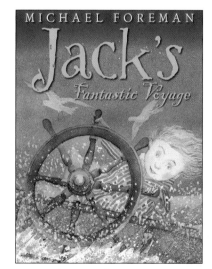

9781849392563